A LOW GROWL RATTLED
IN SEBASTIAN'S THROAT . . .

Slowly, silently, the window slid up. A hand with many rings appeared on the sill. Now the other hand appeared. It held a jeweled knife. It was Marco, the angry Gypsy!

Sebastian nudged Meemew, urging her to follow him. But the cat suddenly sprang toward the open window, shrieking in a high cat yell. Marco's hand reached out and caught Meemew in midair.

Marco had Meemew and he was climbing into a car. The wiggling cat was wailing like a siren.

Why did the Gypsy take Old Tuna Breath?

Like it or not, Sebastian must save that stupid cat, save her from that terrible knife-wielding Gypsy, Marco. But how?

Mary Blount Christian

SEBASTIAN (Super Sleuth) and the Hair of the Dog Mystery

Illustrated by LISA McCUE

A BANTAM SKYLARK BOOK®
TORONTO · NEW YORK · LONDON · SYDNEY · AUCKLAND

RL5, 008–011

SEBASTIAN (SUPER SLEUTH) AND
THE HAIR OF THE DOG MYSTERY

*A Bantam Book / published by arrangement with
Macmillan Publishing Co., Inc.*

PRINTING HISTORY

Macmillan Publishing edition published October 1982

*Skylark Books is a registered trademark of Bantam Books, Inc.
Registered in U.S. Patent and Trademark Office and elsewhere.*

*Bantam Skylark edition / October 1984
2nd printing . . . February 1987*

*Bantam Books are published by Bantam Books, Inc. Its trademark, consisting
of the words "Bantam Books" and the portrayal of a rooster, is Registered
in U.S. Patent and Trademark Office and in other countries. Marca Regis-
trada. Bantam Books, Inc., 666 Fifth Avenue, New York, New York 10103.*

PRINTED IN THE UNITED STATES OF AMERICA

CW   11 10 9 8 7 6 5 4 3 2

Remembering Popsicle, Scarabee, Sable, Tiger, Dawg, Singdoodle, and Tom, who loved us unconditionally and brought joy into our lives for all too brief a time, and with gratitude for Necromancy, who still does.

Contents

1
The Night Visitor

Sebastian sprawled across the length of John's old green couch. His paws twitched rhythmically as he dreamed of chasing a bank robber through the downtown streets while frightened pedestrians screamed, "Look! It's Super Dog!"

But just when he got to the good part where he won the Hero Dog of the Year Award there was a sudden brash buzz of the doorbell.

Sebastian sprang to his feet. Raaa-*ruff*! he snapped. He wanted John to know that he was on guard. And he wanted to alert whoever was on the other side of that door that he would tolerate no trouble—no trouble at all.

John opened the door and stepped back in surprise. "Uh . . . why . . . uh . . . Chief! What are *you* doing here?" he blurted out. "Uh . . . that is . . . I mean—is there something wrong?"

The beetle-browed Chief of Police scowled. Sebastian wondered if the old grump's face would crack if he ever smiled. Not that there was any danger of that, he supposed.

"No. Nothing is really wrong. That is, I . . . I . . . ." Chief sounded almost embarrassed. Sebastian leaned back on his haunches. He was going to enjoy this scene.

His keen eyes noticed that Chief carried a large case covered with a cloth. A present, maybe? Probably Chief wanted to apologize for all those nasty things he'd said about Sebastian.

Sebastian licked his lips. Maybe it was a case of hamburgers, or even a big juicy roast!

"I have to leave town for the weekend," Chief said. "You remember—the police chiefs' conference on crime, in New York?" He hesitated again, staring at his own feet. "I have tried everyone I can think of. You are my absolute last resort, Detective John Quincy Jones—John. She gets so nervous at kennels that she sheds for months—I just can't do that to her again. I'd like to leave her with you."

Chief whipped the cover from the case. Sebastian's jaw dropped.

A cat! The chief was bringing a cat right into *his* very own living room! And he was asking them to keep it for an entire weekend. What if the other

dogs in the neighborhood got wind of a cat here? Why, they'd think the old master was losing his touch! How unbearable—a fluffy, purry, forever-washing-itself cat!

"Come on, little babykins," Chief cooed. "Come to Daddy. Don't be afraid. Nummy, num, num, num."

Chief held out the bundle of long white fur. Then he seemed to remember that John and Sebastian were watching. He cleared his throat.

"This is Meemew," he said proudly.

Sebastian thought he'd be sick. That name! And imagine talking to a dumb cat like that. Ick! Wouldn't you just know that Chief would have a cat instead of a dog? he thought smugly. It figures!

"Isn't she cute?" Chief asked, almost glowing with pride. "And she can do tricks, too. Watch! Come here, babykins."

Chief held out a collar of shiny blue beads. The cat walked up and stuck her head through it, then wiggled until the collar settled around her neck.

"I bet that silly dog of yours can't put on *his* collar!" Chief gloated.

Sebastian yawned to show his distaste for these gaudy show business tactics. He should have known Chief would teach his silly cat such useless tricks. Could she solve a mystery? Could she disguise herself as anything but a ball of fur? How could he compare a silly cat to Sebastian (Super Sleuth), the greatest dog detective of all time?

Meemew stretched and yawned smugly, then ran her pink tongue across one of her paws.

"I *know* how that beast of yours eats," Chief said, glaring at Sebastian accusingly. "You make sure he stays out of Meemew's food now."

John gave Sebastian a tender little pat on the head. "Oh, babykins—uh, I mean, Meemew—

4

needn't worry about this big fella, right, boy?"

Sebastian gave a weak wag of his tail. After all, it was John's detective job with the police force that kept them in hamburgers and, besides, gave Sebastian the chance to keep his own fantastic detective skills in fine tune. He would just have to make the best of it, no matter how humiliating it was.

Chief set Meemew down. Slowly she approached Sebastian, her green eyes staring steadily at him.

She rubbed against him, then her fluffy tail paused before flicking the end of his sensitive nose.

Sebastian sneezed. He curled his lip so that his teeth showed white. A slow growl rumbled deep inside his throat.

"If that brute of a dog hurts my little Meemew. . . ." Chief muttered.

"Oh, now don't be hasty," John pleaded. "Sebastian's just sort of *talking* to the cat. They'll get along just fine, really."

Sebastian immediately looked hangdog and meekly wagged his tail—he knew how to play the game.

When all was calm Chief continued. "Here's her food. Shrimp and tuna with lots of nice sauce. And she likes her milk slightly warmed," he added.

By now Meemew had begun to knead and fluff Sebastian's fur into a comfortable bed for herself.

She purred loudly and blinked her big green eyes at him.

Oh, misery! Sebastian thought. How could he stand this for a whole weekend? Meemew dug one claw deep into his sensitive skin. Oh, pain! Are our detective jobs really worth all this? he wondered.

Chief turned to leave, obviously content that his little Meemew was in adequate, if not competent hands. "Oh, by the way, Detective Jones. The Gypsy Folk Dance Company is in town for three performances at the Folk Theater. A rare emerald necklace belonging to the Gypsy princess is stored in the downtown police station vault. She wears the necklace during each performance.

"Just before curtain time I want you to take the necklace to her and stand guard for the length of each performance. It'll be your job to see that no harm comes to the necklace during their three-day stay."

John nodded. Chief cleared his throat. "Uh, these Gypsies are a little superstitious, so watch what you say and do," he warned in a somber tone.

Sebastian wagged his tail excitedly. It would be wonderful to see the Gypsies perform their colorful, happy dances. And great to get away from that fur ball Meemew, too. But he did wonder what Chief meant by their superstitions.

Well, never mind that now, he thought. If he was going to help John guard the emerald necklace he'd need to keep up his strength.

He trotted into the kitchen, wondering if Mee-mew's tuna with sauce was as tasty as it sounded.

2

Some Hair of the Dog That Bit Him

When Sebastian reached the kitchen Meemew was already at her bowl, nibbling. A speck here. A smidgin there. Why can't cats *eat* instead of being so picky? he wondered.

He settled down at his own bowl and with a few healthy gulps finished his meal. Meemew finally walked to a corner of the kitchen and began washing herself.

Sebastian slipped his pink tongue into her bowl and devoured the remains of tasty tuna and sauce with one flick of his tongue.

Now, that's the way to eat! he thought.

"Come on, big fella," John called. "It's time to go. Sorry, Meemew. You'll have to stay here."

His nose at a proper height to show silly Meemew

who really counted around *this* house, Sebastian trotted out and hopped into John's car.

When they'd picked up the necklace at the police station he and John drove directly to the theater. Backstage there was a flurry of color and excitement.

Bangles, bells and clanging jewelry made a steady tinkling noise as the dancers hurried to take their places. Some of them practiced spins and leaps. A few men in wide pantaloons and high black boots pushed a wagon onto the stage. A fake campfire was already at center stage.

Several men wearing colorful scarves were tuning their violins. The shrill sound hurt Sebastian's ears. He gritted his teeth and fought the terrible urge to howl.

John and Sebastian made their way through the crowd of dancers to the dressing rooms. At the door with a star on it John knocked. A young Gypsy woman was tying a print scarf around her dark hair as she greeted them.

John flushed and introduced himself to the Gypsy princess. He handed the box to her.

She flashed a smile at him. "I am Nadja," she said huskily. She took a key from around her neck, unlocked the box and pulled out a string of green beads.

Nadja fluttered her lashes at John and waved the string of emeralds gently in front of him.

"They are *most* valuable. They mean *much* to my tribe. I have *never* danced without them. It is a superstition—much bad luck will come if I do not dance with them."

Sebastian yawned. They looked pretty much like the beads that Meemew wore for a collar, except these were green like Meemew's eyes. He sniffed around the room. There were flowers everywhere. Why didn't people send meat for good wishes instead of useless flowers?

The audience had already gathered. The lights backstage blinked several times.

"That is a signal that it is time for the folk dances to begin," Nadja told John. "Why do you not sit in the wings and watch?"

John carried a folding chair close to the stage, just out of sight of the audience. The Gypsy woman flashed John another smile. He blushed.

Sebastian sighed and sprawled on the floor close to John. The dancers flashed by him, clicking and jangling and snapping their fingers and leaping into the air. The violins grew louder and sadder as the dances went on.

Despite all he could do to suppress it Sebastian felt a whimper growing into a howl, much like the sounds of the violins. His body trembled as he bravely fought it.

"No, boy!" John scolded.

Sebastian thought it'd be best if he waited outside until the performance was completed. He didn't want to embarrass John with his howling, but what was a dog to do? How could he resist? He went out and waited in the alley.

After a while people poured from the theater. Sebastian made his way back to Nadja's dressing room. He found John already there, talking and laughing with the princess.

He was about to be upset over the attention those two were giving each other, when he spotted another man. He wore a printed cloth around his head. He had rings and bracelets on and in one ear he wore a golden earring. Sebastian suddenly realized that all the Gypsies wore one golden earring each.

Then his sensitive nose picked up the scent of a

chicken salad sandwich. There! There was the lovely sandwich just lying on a plate near where the man's hand rested.

No one seemed to be paying any attention to the sandwich. Why should it go to waste? he asked himself. Then he answered himself: It shouldn't. He opened his mouth to grab the sandwich.

But just as he snapped at the sandwich, the man reached for it, too. Before Sebastian could release his grip the man jerked his hand back and Sebastian felt his teeth break the skin.

"Iiiieeeee!" the man yowled. "Yiiii! Mad dog! Werewolf!"

The man stared down at his hand. There were tiny tooth marks and a small trickle of blood. "I'm *bleeding!*" he shouted. Then he fainted.

By now the other dancers had gathered outside the door, peering in. "What's happened?" someone asked.

"Oh, it's Marco," Alexi, one of the dancers, told them. He threw back his head and laughed broadly. "Our great chief! He has fainted!"

Laughter rose. But Nadja looked frightened. "You'd better get your doggie out of here," she told John. "Marco will be furious when he awakens. Already he's threatened by Alexi, who wants to be chieftain. And now he's in disgrace before the tribe for fainting.

"He is terribly old fashioned," she explained. "He will want some of the hair of the dog that bit him." Nadja looked in every direction, then spoke softly. "And he won't be particular *how* he gets that hair, either."

Sebastian felt his skin prickle. What did Nadja mean by that? Would the man try to hurt him? Could the great Super Sleuth be in danger?

John rummaged through his billfold. "It was just an accident, I'm sure. Sebastian's quite healthy. See? Here is his rabies certificate. He wasn't trying to bite Marco. I suspect they just reached for that sandwich at the same time. I'm sure of it. Sebastian is just hungry, poor old thing."

Suddenly the impact of what Nadja had said must've finally reached John. "And, see here, Princess. What do you mean, Marco doesn't care how he gets the hair?"

Nadja put her fingers to her lips to indicate silence. Then she pointed to a jeweled knife stuck in Marco's belt.

Sebastian felt a quiver run up his spine. Did she mean that man might try to *scalp* him?

"Here," Nadja said, handing the emerald necklace to John. "Take these back to your police vault until the next show. I will bathe Marco's hand. But you had best go—now!"

By then the theater manager had sent a doctor

backstage. He looked at Sebastian's certificate and nodded. "That's fine," he said. "It's just a minor scratch. I'll give him a tetanus shot to be safe." The doctor took a hypodermic needle from his black bag.

Just then Marco came to and saw the needle aimed at him. He fainted again.

There were jeers and laughter just outside the door. Alexi said, "Perhaps it is time to get a *new* leader—one who is not such a scared little bunny. Someone brave, like me!"

"Now he will be doubly mad," Nadja said in almost a whisper. "You had best get your doggie and leave before he comes to. Hurry!"

She didn't have to convince Sebastian. But on the way out he scooped the sandwich into his mouth and swallowed quickly. No use in leaving it around. It would only remind Marco to be mad, Sebastian decided. He trotted out to the car, where John joined him.

"Well, now we know what the chief meant about these Gypsies being superstitious, don't we, old boy?" John asked.

"I guess I had better keep you home for the next few days. I'll finish this assignment alone. No telling how that Gypsy is going to feel when he wakes up. And you might look funny scalped bald," John said, chuckling.

Sebastian swallowed hard. It was going to be awful having to stay home with Old Tuna Breath. But in his mind he could see that shiny knife aimed right at him.

3
Shadow, Shadow on the Wall

All the next day Sebastian had the strange feeling that he was being watched. At the grocery store. At the hamburger drive-in, and even at the laundromat. He couldn't shake the quivery feeling that ran up and down his back.

It upset him so much, in fact, that he ate both his and John's hamburgers, a box of chocolates John had bought for Nadja and half of a steak advertisement in the evening paper.

When John went to the Folk Theater Saturday night he left Sebastian home with Meemew. "Sorry, old man," he apologized. "But we had better avoid that angry Gypsy like the fleas." John chuckled, then left.

Sometimes Sebastian had trouble with John's brand of humor. There was nothing funny about fleas. And there was nothing funny about that crazy

16

Gypsy wanting to scalp him, either. And he didn't particularly like leaving John alone with that princess flashing her eyes at him, either.

John had turned out all the lights. "It'll look as if we're all gone," he'd said.

Sebastian felt it would be better to have at least a night light, but try as he would he couldn't nudge the light switch on. And he dared not try the table lamp. The last time he broke it—and it took John three weeks to mend it. It still leaned at a funny angle.

He sighed and settled down on the couch to dog-nap until John's return. Meemew soon curled up close to his warm tummy and purred softly. Blast that stupid cat, Sebastian thought as he drifted into sleep. He hoped that Chief would decide to come home early from the conference.

Suddenly Sebastian felt that strange prickle on his neck again, the same feeling he'd had when he thought someone was watching him. A low growl rattled deep in his throat.

Meemew's fur stiffened the length of her spine and her tail looked double its normal size.

Slowly he surveyed the shadows in the room with his sharp eyes. One shadow moved.

Sebastian peered cautiously over the arm of the couch at the window. There was the shadow of a

man. The moonlight caught the glint of one golden earring.

Meemew was bleating like a lamb. "Maa-maa."

Sebastian nudged her with his nose, hoping she'd be quiet. But she spat furiously.

Slowly, silently, the window slid up. A hand with many rings appeared on the sill. Now the other hand appeared. It held a jeweled knife. It was Marco, the angry Gypsy.

Sebastian nudged Meemew, urging her to follow him. Carefully he slipped from the couch, and keeping in the shadows, crept toward the half-opened closet.

But Meemew didn't follow. She was still on the couch. The window was all the way open now. The dark figure slid inside. Meemew suddenly sprang toward the open window, shrieking in a high cat yell.

There was a loud crash as the lamp fell. Marco's hand reached out and caught Meemew in midair.

Sebastian crouched, ready to leap at the Gypsy. But he didn't come. Sebastian peered from the closet. The room was empty.

He stepped lightly over the broken lamp, ran to the window and looked out. Marco had Meemew and he was climbing into a car. The wiggling Meemew was wailing like a siren.

Sebastian stared at the departing car. Maybe Marco had grabbed at Meemew in the dark, thinking she was actually the old Super Sleuth. But he certainly would know the difference by now, so why did he carry off Old Tuna Breath?

Nadja had said Marco didn't care how he got the hair of the dog, so long as he gained favor with his tribe once more. Maybe he didn't even care if it *was* the hair of the *dog*. Meemew's fur was about the same color as his own.

Was Marco *that* desperate? Was he going to scalp Meemew and fool his tribe? Marco was not a nice man, Sebastian decided.

With John gone and Chief depending on them to take care of Meemew, he, Sebastian (Super Sleuth), would have to take charge, even if he didn't like her.

At least he wouldn't be home when John found that broken lamp! he consoled himself. Ah, well. Heaving a mighty sigh, Sebastian sprang from the house through the open window. He raced through the streets toward the Folk Theater.

Like it or not, he must save that stupid cat, save her from that terrible knife-wielding Gypsy, Marco. But how?

4
Dance, Gypsy, Sing, Gypsy!

When Sebastian reached the Folk Theater he was relieved to find that the violins were not being tuned. There was only the usual bustle backstage. The dancers were already dressed and running around, screeching instructions to each other.

He did not see John. That was lucky. He didn't know what John would say if he saw him. Cautiously Sebastian kept to the shadows—no need to arouse suspicion. He had to find Meemew, and, he hoped, before that Marco could chop off her fur. Poor Meemew!

He heard cooing noises coming from Nadja's dressing room. His heart leaped in fear. Was Nadja saying sweet things to John? She'd better not be!

Luckily he was just keyhole height. As casually as he could, Sebastian peeked through.

Nadja was talking softly, but he could not see

21

to whom. "You are such a little darling. You are so very beau-ti-ful! Kootch, kootcha, little one. Oh, my precious one."

When Nadja leaned back to look at herself in the mirror Sebastian saw. It was Meemew! She was on Nadja's dressing table, purring and writhing while Nadja sweet-talked her. Stupid cat!

She didn't even look like she was in danger. Sebastian backed away. Maybe Meemew *wasn't* the one in danger. Maybe Marco had known all along that Sebastian, the bravest of all canines, would follow and try to save her. Maybe this was a trap!

He turned to leave when he spotted Marco coming toward him. Quickly Sebastian ducked through a door. There were racks and racks of Gypsy costumes hanging in the room. He eyed them thoughtfully.

If he was going to get out of this alive—with all his fur intact—he was going to have to disguise himself. But what disguise could the master of disguises use? It is so hard to continually top oneself! he sighed. He'd been a fur coat in the closet of that movie star, finally cracking The Case of the Missing Muskrat Coat. And he'd been a bearskin rug at the ski lodge, solving The Case of the Skewered Skiier, and—ummm . . . .

Seizing one of the costumes that hung before him, Sebastian quickly wriggled into it. He nudged at one of the bandanas until he settled it properly over his head. He quickly slipped into two pairs of boots, then discarded the front pair. Stupid mistakes like that could cost him his identity—and his scalp.

When he came from the costume room he was confident that no one would recognize him—not even John. To all who would see him he was a lovely Gypsy girl, a member of the dance company.

Sebastian crept toward the backstage exit. He

could worry about getting the costume back later. Right now he had to get out of there.

But before he had walked even six feet a gruff voice called.

"Hey, you!"

Sebastian froze in his path. How had Marco guessed? What had given him away? Was his tail showing? Well, he would face his fate like the noble dog he was.

"Gypsy girl," Marco said, softer this time. "Get ready. The dancers are about to begin."

Sebastian nodded. So be it. He would have to go through with the disguise. He trotted toward the

stage and someone handed him a tambourine. He seized it between his teeth just as the curtains parted and the music began.

The dance company leaped to the stage, with Sebastian in the middle, leaping as high, perhaps higher, than the rest. He was so glad he'd watched when John was taking those disco lessons. And of course his own natural grace was an asset.

The tambourines rattled and here and there the Gypsies yelled "Hi-yiii!" as they leaped.

And then it happened. Just what Sebastian had dreaded. The violins began their low and soulful whine. He gripped the tambourine tightly between

his teeth. He must fight it, he told himself. He *must*!

The violins grew louder and higher. At last he could hold back no longer.

Dropping his tambourine to the stage Sebastian threw back his head and howled a long and satisfying "Ah-OOOOoooooo," trying desperately to keep in tune.

The audience gasped almost as one.

"Bravo!" someone screamed. "Bravo!"

Louder and louder he wailed. The Gypsies whirled and leaped wilder and wilder. They swayed and waved their arms to the music. Nadja, the emeralds shimmering around her neck, whirled and spun and leaped, too. She smiled and flashed her eyes.

The violins grew more and more sorrowful. Sebastian howled louder. "Ah-*OOoooOOoooo*."

Suddenly Marco yelled, "Stop!"

The violins hushed. The audience hushed. The other Gypsies stopped. Sebastian stopped in mid-"ooo" and stared. Marco was pointing at him!

"Impostor!" Marco yelled. "This one is not of Gypsy blood."

The other Gypsies drew back in alarm. "Oooohhh!" one cried. "Look! She *is* an impostor."

Sebastian looked from one face to another. How? How could they see through his excellent disguise? Why did he look any different from them? And then it came to him in a flash.

Stupid, stupid mistake! he scolded himself. Of course. He *did* look different from the rest of them. He had forgotten to put on one golden earring!

The Gypsies circled him, slowly at first, then more swiftly. They surrounded him and began moving closer. They were going to catch him—unless—

Sebastian sprang. Over the heads of the Gypsies, into the audience he ran. Swiftly he rushed down the red-carpeted aisles with the Gypsies close behind.

The audience cheered wildly. "Bravo! Bravo!"

"How realistic! How typically Gypsy!" a woman cooed at Sebastian as he raced past her.

He saw John in the audience, applauding as wildly as the rest. He shouted, "More! More!"

Sebastian knew now he couldn't count on John to help. His master, like the others, thought this was part of the act.

Sebastian brushed through the lobby, kicking off the boots as he ran. Outside on the steps he shook the bandana from his head. And around the corner in the alley he jumped from the skirt and peasant blouse.

At least he needn't worry about returning the costume, he thought, panting. Those Gypsies were close behind and they'd gather it up. Just so *he* wasn't in it.

Exactly as he thought they would, the Gypsies stopped long enough to gather the clothes, giving Sebastian time to leap into an open garbage can in back of the Pizza House.

"Who could it have been?" he heard Marco ask aloud.

"Look at this bandana, Chieftain," one of the men said. "There's white hair."

Marco scratched his chin. "Continue to search the streets," he said, waving the discarded clothes. "We are looking for either an old lady in her petticoat or a clever Gypsy-biting dog."

The Gypsies divided and searched the alley. Sebastian trembled as they neared his hiding place.

Sebastian figured that now he was a gone dog for sure. But just as Marco neared his garbage can a Gypsy woman ran into the alley.

"Marco! Marco, come quickly! The emerald necklace—it is gone. Someone has stolen it!"

5
Anchovies!

Quietly Sebastian waited. When the alley was again silent he crawled from the garbage can.

Sebastian sniffed himself. Of all the places to have to hide! In the garbage can of a pizza place! He was covered with tomato paste, mozzarella shavings and anchovies. It made his eyes water.

He shook, sending pastry flakes and leftovers flying in every direction. Well, he thought, he couldn't waste time worrying about his appearance.

Chief would be doubly furious now. That crazy cat whisked away from John's apartment, and now the necklace missing. He, Sebastian (Super Sleuth), would have to help John get both of them back to their rightful places. At least he knew where that cat was. He would have to return to the theater, of course. And that would be dangerous.

That nutty Gypsy was still on the lookout for him

and his fur. And not even a golden earring would be a good enough disguise to get him in there now. They would certainly be more cautious than before.

He'd have to use a different disguise, but what? Sebastian sniffed his fur again. Those leftovers did smell pretty good, except for the anchovies. And they did give him an idea.

He nudged open the service entrance to the Pizza House. On a hook he saw an apron and a chef's hat with PIZZA HOUSE written in red across it. That would do nicely.

Just as he wiggled into the new disguise the cook stuck his head in. "You the new delivery boy?"

"Ummm." Sebastian made a throaty growl.

"Good. There's some ready to go. Here are the addresses. Boy! You smell like you fell into the anchovy barrel. Phew!"

The cook went back into the kitchen, humming.

Good, Sebastian thought, he doesn't suspect a thing. Sebastian wolfed down one of the pizzas first, then seized the boxed ones between his teeth and trotted into the alley and up the street toward the Folk Theater.

There was a lot of commotion going on when he got there. John had his notebook out and was questioning Nadja. Sebastian eavesdropped.

"But, darling policeman," she said, "the necklace was right here in my dressing room. I was playing with the darling little kitty cat after the performance. I hung my necklace on this jewelry tree," she said, waving her arm toward a metal holder on her dressing table.

"I changed my costume behind that screen and when I looked back the necklace was gone. And so was the darling kitty cat."

Oh, no! Sebastian thought, the cat is gone again. Now he had two problems to solve. He put the pizzas on the radiator. At least when he delivered them they'd still be warm.

He edged closer to the crowd in Nadja's dressing room.

"Just give me a little while to find the necklace before calling the station," John pleaded. "Maybe I can find it and Chief won't ever have to know—I mean, be worried."

But Marco was furious. "No! It is that dog! I know it is that dog. It is the Gypsy curse. The necklace will not be returned."

Alexi laughed. "Old bunny rabbit!" he jeered at Marco.

Marco's eyes burned. "You'll see," he snarled.

Nadja said, "Please, Marco. Give the lovely policeman until morning. Just until morning. Perhaps he can work miracles that your hair-of-the-dog spell cannot."

Marco nodded. "Very well, for you, Princess. Until the moon sets. That is all the time you have."

John, still blushing at Nadja's reference to him, nodded. "I'll do my best. Thank you," he murmured.

He took out his kit and dusted for fingerprints. Sebastian pulled back into the shadows. It is time for the master sleuth to think, he told himself.

Perhaps it was Marco who took the necklace. He was about to lose the chieftainship of his tribe. He was angry and even a little frightened. Perhaps he has hidden the necklace and plans to bring it out at the right moment to regain favor with his people, the cunning canine cleverly deduced.

Or did Alexi take it? He was most anxious to be chieftain himself. Perhaps he hoped to win the affection of the tribe by recovering the necklace.

Sebastian thought that maybe even Nadja could have taken the necklace. He didn't trust anybody who made eyes at his master like that! Perhaps this was her way of getting attention from John. Besides, she liked cats—she couldn't be all that nice!

Or perhaps it could be any one of the Gypsy dancers. Maybe some woman was jealous of Nadja and wanted to be the lead dancer. Or one of the men? Neither Marco or Alexi were particularly lovable. Maybe someone decided that *neither* of them should be chief.

But where was Meemew? She had been in Nadja's dressing room. He'd seen her there, himself. Did Marco take her again? Why? Because she was a witness?

Maybe she just walked out. If someone wasn't cuddling her and cooing at her, she probably got bored. But she'd never find her way back to the apartment and Chief would be furious.

It was up to Super Sleuth. He'd simply have to find her and get her home before he could help John. After all, John couldn't botch things up too much in that little time, could he? And maybe he could finish delivering those pizzas on the way.

Nose to the ground, Sebastian followed Meemew's scent out of the theater and down the street. He was only three blocks away when he spotted her—up a tree. Three dogs were barking and jumping at her.

She was yowling at the top of her lungs and spitting and hissing at them.

Sebastian put the pizzas down and trotted over to help her. Gaaa-*ruff*! he barked.

He cleared his throat and barked again, this time a little louder. Raaaa-*rufff*!

34

The dogs turned to face him. But when they sniffed the anchovies they turned tail and fled.

Sebastian stretched up to try and help Meemew down. Ga-ruff, he told her. But Meemew was still so upset that she spat and struck out at him with her claws.

Ga-*rufffft*, Sebastian urged again. Suddenly he felt a painful jab in his ribs. Had Marco found him? But he turned to see a woman poking him in the ribs with her umbrella.

She poked him again. "Bad dog! Go away!" she scolded. "Leave the sweet little kitty alone."

Sebastian winced as she whacked him over the head with the umbrella.

"Go away!" she shouted again.

Sebastian looked hangdog and retreated. No need to get into an argument with a lady and her umbrella, he figured. He backed up and sat down. Maybe she would go away and then he could get Meemew down.

"That's better," the woman said. She lifted Meemew from the tree. "What a lovely, pretty kitty," she cooed. "And your pretty collar is exactly the color of your lovely eyes.

"Well, you must belong to someone. I'll just take you home with me until I can find your owner."

She kept talking baby talk to Meemew, who

purred her gratitude. Stupid cat, Sebastian thought. Why didn't she just jump down and follow *him* like she ought to?

Well, there was nothing left to do but follow them to the woman's house. Maybe he could figure out a way to get Meemew back. He couldn't bother John. He was too busy looking for that necklace.

"Shooo!" the woman screeched in Sebastian's direction. "I know you are back there, even if I can't see you," she scolded. "I can *smell* you."

The old silent Super Sleuth, detected by a woman with an umbrella! How humiliating! Blasted anchovies, Sebastian thought.

6
To the Rescue!

Sebastian was careful to stay downwind of the woman and Meemew. At last they went into a house. A light went on in the back. Sebastian went around and peeked through the window. The lady had Meemew sitting on a velvet chair.

Meemew was purring and eating little bits of chicken from a spoon. It was disgusting. And here he had come to rescue her. He was half starving and that blasted cat was eating like a queen.

The woman wrinkled her nose and looked toward the window. Sebastian ducked down. He was just in time because she came over and shut the window tight.

Sebastian knew he had to hurry and get Meemew out of there and safely home. Only then could he turn his attention to the necklace.

It would be moonset in a few hours. Then Marco

would tell the police that the necklace was gone. Chief would be told and John would be sent to direct traffic at a cattle crossing or something completely unworthy of Sebastian's masterful skills.

Sebastian spotted a bird bath, which reminded him how thirsty he was. He stood up on the bowl and lapped water. He must have been louder than he thought because before long the outdoor lights went on.

"Eeeek, Henry!" the woman yelled. "It's that awful smelly dog again. He's out at the birdbath. Do something, Henry."

A man—probably Henry, Sebastian cleverly deduced—grabbed the umbrella and ran outside. He waved it and yelled, "Go away. Away! Phew! Anchovies!"

Sebastian ran around and around the birdbath, woofing at the top of his lungs. When he momentarily got ahead of the man he glanced toward the door. That stupid cat was just sitting there, washing her paws and watching the whole scene.

Ga-*rufff*! Sebastian barked. Ga-*rufff*! The cat just kept on licking and watching. Gaaaaaa-*ruffffff*! he barked again.

The man caught up with Sebastian and poked him with the umbrella. Sebastian twitched free and ran close to the cat.

She stopped licking and sniffed. She sniffed again. Anchovies!

Meeeeeeow! she screeched and leaped after Sebastian. Now that he saw that the cat was following him, he took off around the house. Meemew was close behind.

"Hen-ry!" the woman yelled. "You were only supposed to chase off that awful smelly dog. Now that darling cat is gone, too!"

Sebastian collapsed into a panting heap of hair several blocks from the house. He had to catch his breath.

Meemew caught up and licked anchovy from his fur, purring noisily.

When he had rested a few minutes he picked Meemew up by the scruff of her neck and trotted toward home. It would be much faster carrying her, he figured.

As he trotted he went over the list of suspects again. Marco was number one. But Sebastian couldn't be sure whether he felt that way about Marco because the man was so determined to scalp him, or because Marco had more to gain by stealing the necklace.

Suspect number two was certainly Alexi, who stood to be chieftain if Marco continued in such disfavor with his people.

Of course there was Nadja herself. Even

though John was sweet on her, he, Sebastian (Super Sleuth), must face the fact that she could be guilty.

Then there was the lady with the umbrella. Sebastian paused. Now why did he think of the lady with the umbrella? She wasn't even aware of the Folk Dance Company, let alone the emeralds.

Was it something she did, or maybe something she said? But what?

Sebastian traced back through the events with his keen mind. She had poked him with the umbrella and that reminded him of Marco. No, that wouldn't be it. She had taken Meemew, but that wasn't stealing. She had thought she was rescuing the cat. What, then, was it?

Like a quick brown fox it came to him. She had talked about Meemew's eyes and the collar to match. But Meemew's collar is blue, he remembered. And her eyes are green. Green. Emeralds are green. Sebastian pushed Meemew into the light. Her white fur was so long that it almost obscured the collar. But sure enough, there with her blue collar was a green one. The emeralds. I'm so cunning I scare myself, he thought. This should get me the Detective of the Year Award!

So Meemew had been the thief after all. Sebastian suddenly had a beautiful vision of Chief's cat behind bars. He wagged his tail with glee as he thought of Chief finding out he had a jail-bound cat, nabbed for a trick he'd taught her!

Sebastian tried to picture how Meemew had stolen it. Nadja said she'd hung the emeralds on a jewelry tree. That must've been just like Chief holding out Meemew's collar.

Maybe Chief should go to jail, too, as an accessory to the crime, Sebastian thought with delight. It made him feel warm and content to think of it.

Enough of that. He must get Meemew back home and get the necklace to John. He looked at the sky. The moon would set soon. There was no time to take Meemew home. He would carry her and the necklace to the Folk Theater.

But when he arrived with Meemew and the necklace it was Alexi who saw them first. And he obviously spotted the necklace, too. Greedily he grabbed it from Meemew's neck. He wrinkled his nose, glancing at Sebastian. "Anchovies," he said, grimacing.

Alexi left Sebastian and Meemew and shouted into the crowd of Gypsies. "I have found the necklace! I should be your chieftain!"

The Gypsies gathered around patting him on the back and telling him how wonderfully clever he was.

Sebastian was horrified. Alexi was a liar! Would

his people believe him and make him chief? As mean as Marco was, *he* hadn't lied.

John's smile was bigger than anyone's. He was probably just glad he didn't have to tell Chief the necklace was missing. He put the emeralds into the box and promised the Gypsies he'd deliver it to the police station at once.

They, in turn, promised never to reveal that the necklace had ever been missing.

Alexi stood around looking smug. Nadja was flashing her eyes at him. Marco sat slumped unhappily on someone's violin.

Just then John spotted Sebastian and Meemew. "Sebastian!" he scolded. "Shame! You shouldn't have followed me here. And you certainly shouldn't have brought Meemew here. What if something had happened to the poor little kitty? Shame."

How *could* John think this hairy hawkshaw had brought the silly cat here? There was no way to convince him, of course. Instead he held out his paw to shake hands. That trick always got to humans. Eat your heart out, Meemew, he thought smugly.

John laughed and bent to shake his paw, but he pulled back quickly. "Anchovies!" he yelled. "Right after I get this necklace into the vault, I'm giving you a *bath!*"

7

Hair Today, There Tomorrow

After John delivered the necklace to the police station he kept his promise. He put Sebastian in the bathtub and scrubbed away the tomato paste and anchovy smell.

John spread towels on the floor. "How on earth did you get such an awful smell anyway?" he asked. "If only you could talk. Ah, well. Stay on these towels until you're dry, big fella."

It was Sunday. Chief would be coming for Mee-mew soon and the Gypsy Folk Dance Company—including that flirt Nadja—would be giving its last performance. If Sebastian was lucky!

Sebastian stretched out on the towels. John flipped through the Sunday paper. "Hmmm, here's a review of the performance last night by that critic, Tarlton Engham. It says, 'The Gypsy Company brought a splash of gaiety and color to the stage, but the highlight of the evening was the dramatic addition which depicts the Gypsies' discovering an outsider amongst them.

" 'The outsider, played by an unknown, gives the most delightful contralto solo ever and this humble critic says without hesitation that a new star is born.' "

John closed the paper. "That performance was good—really good. But she looked so familiar . . . ."

Sebastian sighed. A contralto? Ah, well.

The doorbell rang. Sebastian rushed to the door with John. Maybe it was Chief and they'd soon be rid of that crazy cat.

But it was Marco. Sebastian slunk behind John as the Gypsy spoke. "I have come to say I am sorry about causing you and your doggie so much worry," he said.

"I confess to you that I have always been afraid of the sight of blood—especially my own. But my tribe did not know this until your dog—" He waved his bandaged hand.

John nodded. "I understand."

Marco continued. "Now my tribe laughs at me. I am a good leader. But they do not think so because I could not get any hair of the dog that bit me for the Gypsy spell. I even tried to make do with the cat. Aha, I said to myself, the fur is the same color, and her teeth are not so big. But then I knew if I was to keep my tribe's trust, I must not cheat. If only . . . ." His voice trailed off.

Sebastian crept into the bathroom. He thought Marco didn't look so fierce now. It was time for this cunning canine to help, he decided. Sebastian picked up his brush. He went into the living room and nudged Marco with it.

Marco jumped at Sebastian's touch. "What is it your big dog wants of me? What is he doing?"

John said, "Well, he just had a bath. Perhaps he wants you to brush him."

"Me? You think he wishes to be friendly with me?" Marco smiled. "Ahhh. Something occurs to me."

John looked hopeful. "What is it, Marco?"

"Could it be that when one brushes a dog some of the hair comes off in the brush?"

John nodded, grinning.

"Ahh," Marco continued, "then could I perhaps get some hair of the dog that bit me without any bloodshed—his or mine?"

Again John nodded. "I believe you're right, by golly! No wonder you are the leader of a great tribe! What an idea!"

Marco brushed Sebastian briskly, whistling a Gypsy tune. "Now, I have taken some hair of the dog myself. I have fulfilled my pledge and I have not lied." Marco winked happily. "And I have done this without hurt."

Sebastian was glad that Marco could probably stay chieftain now. But he did not want Alexi to get away with his lie. He trotted off to get Meemew's brush.

"Look," John said. "Maybe he wants you to brush the cat, now."

Marco looked at the brush. Quickly he pulled something from his pocket. "This was caught in the necklace when Alexi said he found it. It matches the hair in the cat's brush, does it not?"

"Well," John said proudly. "Then it's obvious—Alexi didn't really find the necklace—he lied."

Sebastian wagged his tail. Maybe humans weren't so dumb after all! At last this clever canine was about—

But John broke his train of thought. "It was Meemew! Clever little Meemew found the necklace!"

Meemew pranced back and forth, purring and obviously enjoying her false reputation. Sebastian sank to the floor. He thought he was going to be sick. Humans! What's the use? And cats—stupid cats!

The doorbell rang. This time it was Chief. He scooped Meemew up and stroked her lovingly. Chief chatted about his trip with Marco and John. Happily, no mention was made about the adventures

48

of the past several days. Marco even held his bandaged hand behind him so Chief didn't see or ask questions about it.

Finally Chief said, "Oh, by the way, while it's not my usual policy to cater to that overgrown garbage can you call a dog, I appreciate your keeping my precious little Meemew for the weekend. So I've brought something for Sebastian's horrendous and strange appetite."

Sebastian sat up. Mmm. Maybe roast. Or steak? Or even two steaks!

Chief brought out a familiar looking box from behind him. It had writing in red stamped on the front. Chief continued, "I knew he liked pizza, so I

brought him the extra-large size." As he opened the box he said, "It has—"

Marco and John wrinkled their noses. "We know!" They both burst into laughter. "Anchovies!"

Hastily, and maybe even a little gratefully, Sebastian devoured the pizza with anchovies. He sighed. It was better to have them on the inside than the outside. Anytime!

ABOUT THE AUTHOR

MARY BLOUNT CHRISTIAN has written many popular books for children, including *April Fool, The Devil Take You, Barnabas Beane!,* the Goosehill Gang Mysteries, and the sequels to this book, *Sebastian (Super Sleuth) and the Crummy Yummies Caper* and *Sebastian (Super Sleuth) and the Bone to Pick Mystery.* Her *The Lucky Man,* a Ready-to-Read Book, was named a Best Book of the Year 1979 by *School Library Journal.* Ms. Christian is also the creator and moderator of the syndicated PBS-TV series "Children's Bookshelf" and teaches college writing courses in Houston, Texas, her home.

ABOUT THE ILLUSTRATOR

LISA MCCUE is a talented young illustrator of children's books. A graduate of Southeastern Massachusetts University and Hartford Art School at the University of Hartford, Ms. McCue lives in Tappan, New York.

Now you can have your favorite Choose Your Own Adventure® Series in a variety of sizes. Along with the popular pocket size, Bantam has introduced the Choose Your Own Adventure® series in a Skylark edition and also in Hardcover.

Now not only do you get to decide on how you want your adventures to end, you also get to decide on what size you'd like to collect them in.

SKYLARK EDITIONS

☐	15238	The Circus #1 E. Packard	$1.95
☐	15207	The Haunted House #2 R. A. Montgomery	$1.95
☐	15208	Sunken Treasure #3 E. Packard	$1.95
☐	15233	Your Very Own Robot #4 R. A. Montgomery	$1.95
☐	15308	Gorga, The Space Monster #5 E. Packard	$1.95
☐	15309	The Green Slime #6 S. Saunders	$1.95
☐	15195	Help! You're Shrinking #5 E. Packard	$1.95
☐	15201	Indian Trail #8 R. A. Montgomery	$1.95
☐	15191	The Genie In the Bottle #10 J. Razzi	$1.95
☐	15222	The Big Foot Mystery #11 L. Sonberg	$1.95
☐	15223	The Creature From Millers Pond #12 S. Saunders	$1.95
☐	15226	Jungle Safari #13 E. Packard	$1.95
☐	15227	The Search For Champ #14 S. Gilligan	$1.95
☐	15241	Three Wishes #15 S. Gilligan	$1.95
☐	15242	Dragons! #16 J. Razzi	$1.95
☐	15261	Wild Horse Country #17 L. Sonberg	$1.95
☐	15262	Summer Camp #18 J. Gitenstein	$1.95
☐	15270	The Tower of London #19 S. Saunders	$1.95
☐	15271	Trouble In Space #20 J. Woodcock	$1.95

Prices and availability subject to change without notice.

Buy them at your local bookstore or use this handy coupon for ordering:

SPECIAL
MONEY SAVING
OFFER

Now you can have an up-to-date listing of Bantam's hundreds of titles plus take advantage of our unique and exciting bonus book offer. A special offer which gives you the opportunity to purchase a Bantam book for only 50¢. Here's how!

By ordering any five books at the regular price per order, you can also choose any other single book listed (up to a $4.95 value) for just 50¢. Some restrictions do apply, but for further details why not send for Bantam's listing of titles today!

Just send us your name and address plus 50¢ to defray the postage and handling costs.